DAN THE BIGGEST DUMP TRUCK

STORY BY
CHRIS ADAMS

ILLUSTRATED BY
JAMES DONAHOWER

muddy boots™

we jump in puddles

GUILFORD, CONNECTICUT

Dan was the biggest dump truck in the whole wide world.

He was **massive!**

He was **mega-big!**

He was **mighty!**

His tipper could hold one hundred elephants in its bed!

His wheels were as big as houses!

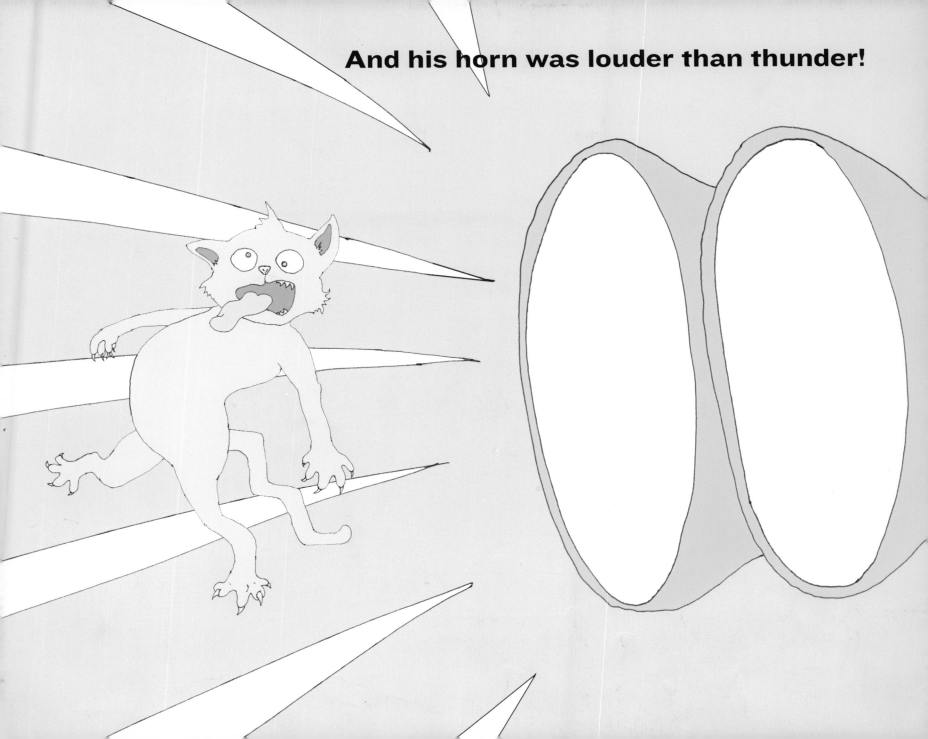

But Dan was lonely.

All he wanted was a construction crew
to call his very own.

One day, Dan went to the skyscraper
construction site.

And all the workers and all the trucks and all the diggers and all the cranes came over to see him.

But when they saw how big he was, they said, "Man oh man, Dan, you're **MUCH** too big to work here!"

So Dan went away, and he was sad.

Then Dan went to the bridge construction site.

And all the workers and all the trucks and all the diggers and all the cranes came over to see him.

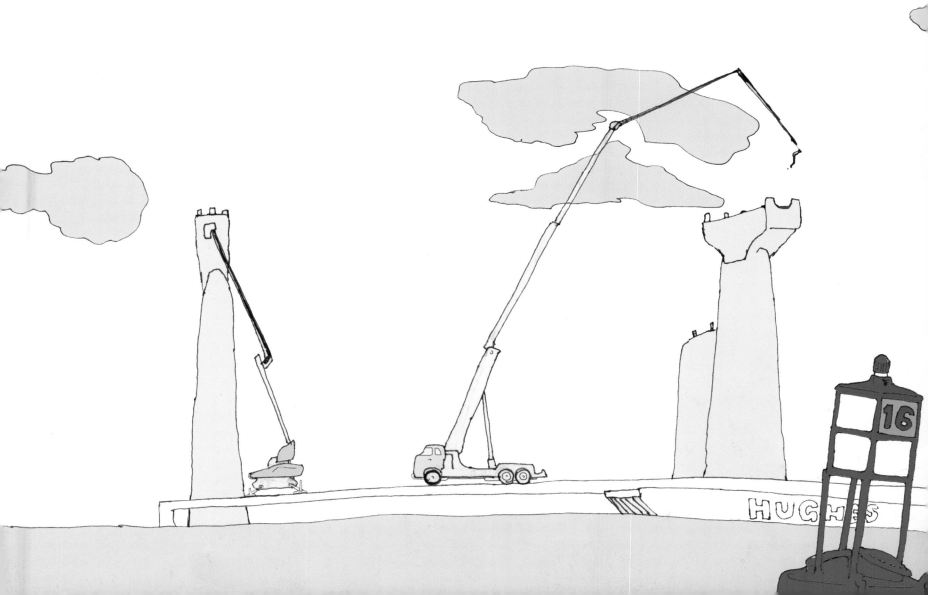

But when they saw how big he was, they said,
"Man oh man, Dan, you're MUCH too big to work here!"

So Dan went away, and he was sad.

Then Dan went to the housing construction site.

And all the workers and all the trucks and all the diggers and all the cranes came over to see him.

But when they saw how big he was, they said,
"Man oh man, Dan, you're **MUCH** too big to work here!"

So Dan went away, and he was sad.

Then the new sports stadium job came to town.

And **ALL** the construction vehicles and **ALL** the construction workers were needed at the site to do the job.

The diggers dug, and the mixers mixed, and the haulers hauled, and the cranes hoisted, and the forklifts lifted, and the bulldozers moved the earth, and the job was going well . . .

Until . . . all that digging and mixing and hauling and hoisting and lifting and earth moving made **SO** much dirt and rocks and rubble that all the trucks and vehicles and the workers and equipment were stuck inside the site!

They had dug so much that there was no way out!

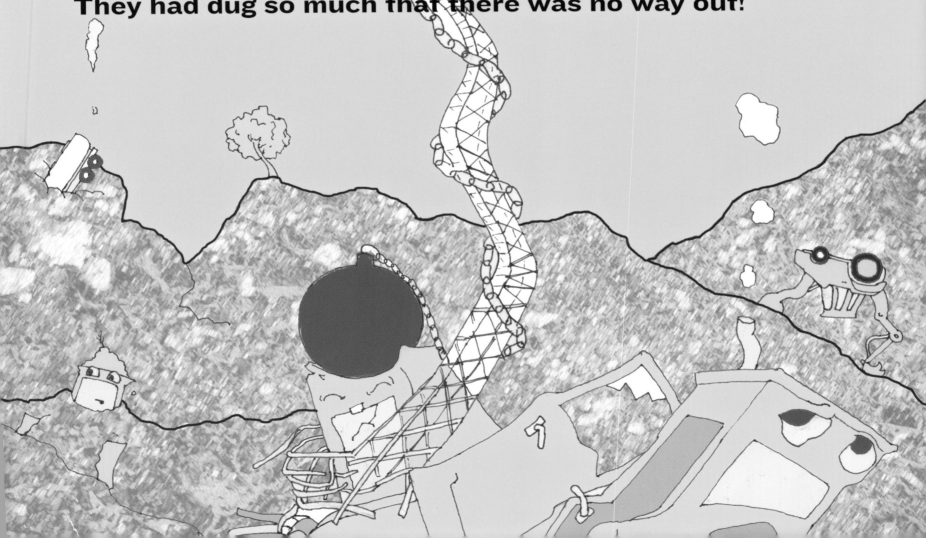

Soon, word spread of the crisis. News vans and reporters arrived on the scene:

"Breaking news—construction crews, trucks, and equipment stuck at the site of the new sports stadium! The foreman is asking that anyone that can help get rid of all the dirt come to the site immediately!"

Dan was driving along, feeling sad, when he heard the news flash on his radio.

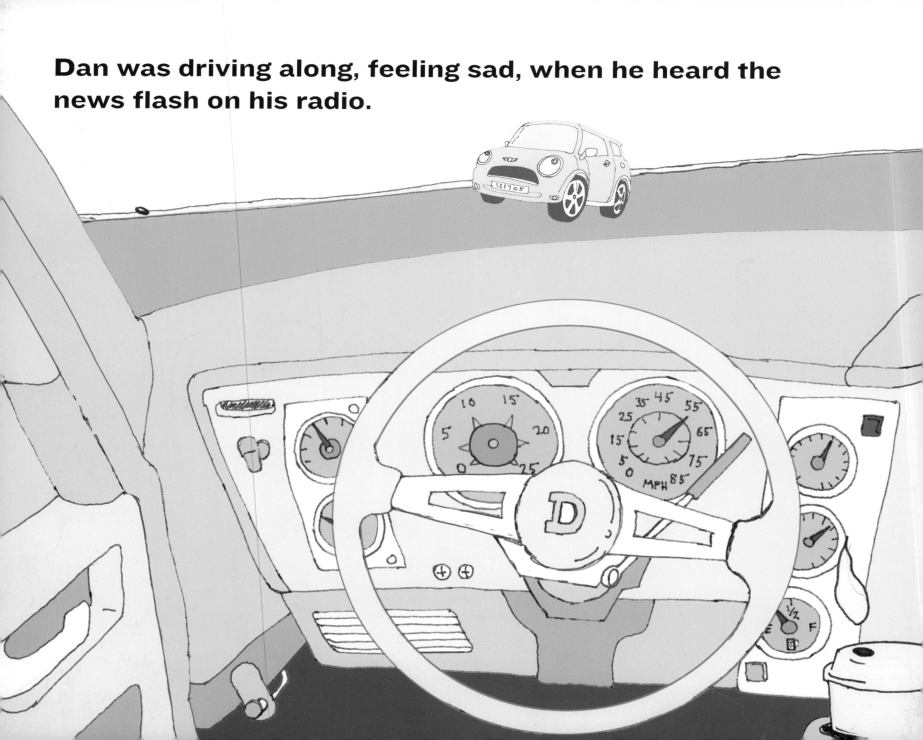

He stopped. And he said to himself, "I can do this!"

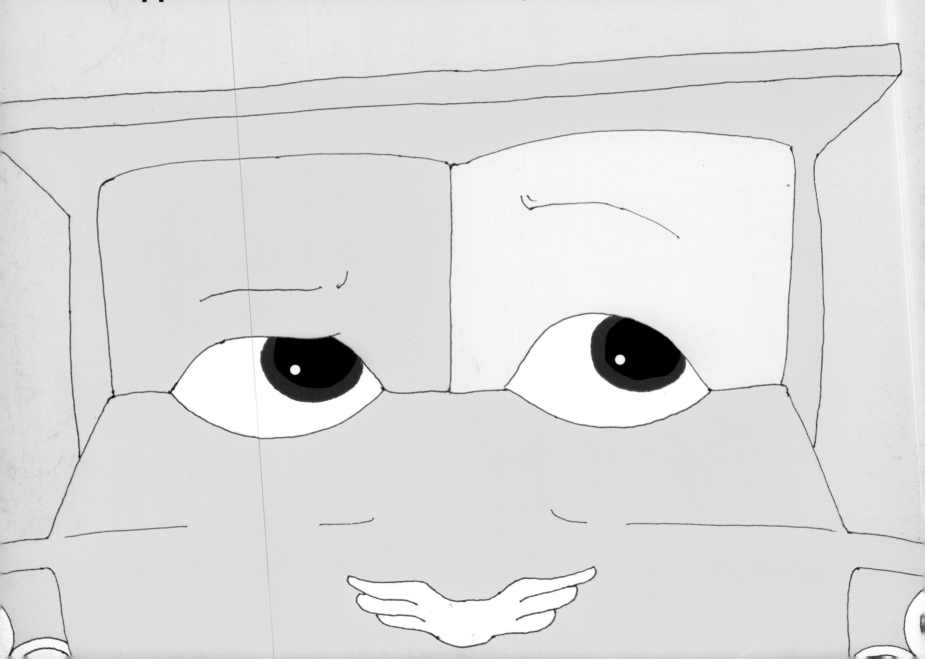

So Dan started up his massive, mighty mega-engine—

BRUMMMM!
BRUMMMM!

And he readied his huge, enormous, gigantic tipper—WHRRRRRRRRRRRRRR!

And he blared his super-loud horns—HONK! HONK!

Dan drove to the job site, shouting out, "Everyone, let me through!"

And when he got to the sports stadium, Dan got to work.

He told the diggers to fill up his tipper with dirt.

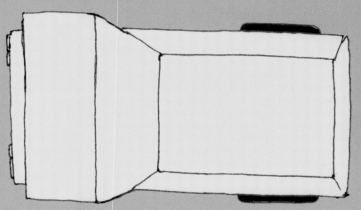

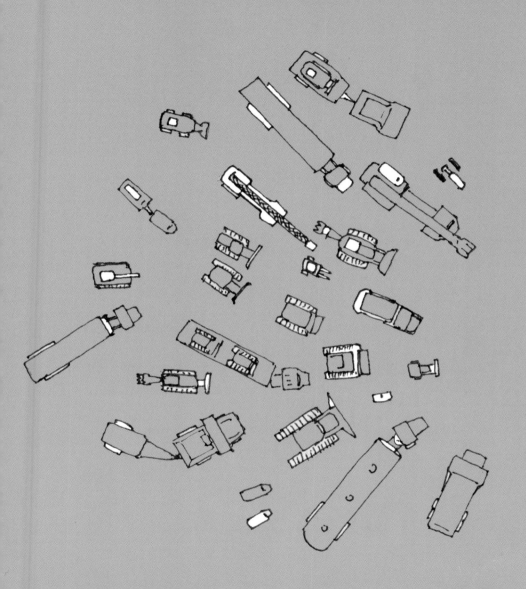

He told the workers to shovel in the rocks.

He told the cranes to put in all the rubble.

So the diggers dug and the workers shoveled and the cranes lifted and all the dirt and all the rocks and all the rubble went into Dan's enormous tipper.

Then Dan started up his engines—

BRUMMMM!
BRUMMMM!

He honked his huge horns—HONK! **HONK!**

His massive tires gripped the road, and
Dan hauled all the dirt away!

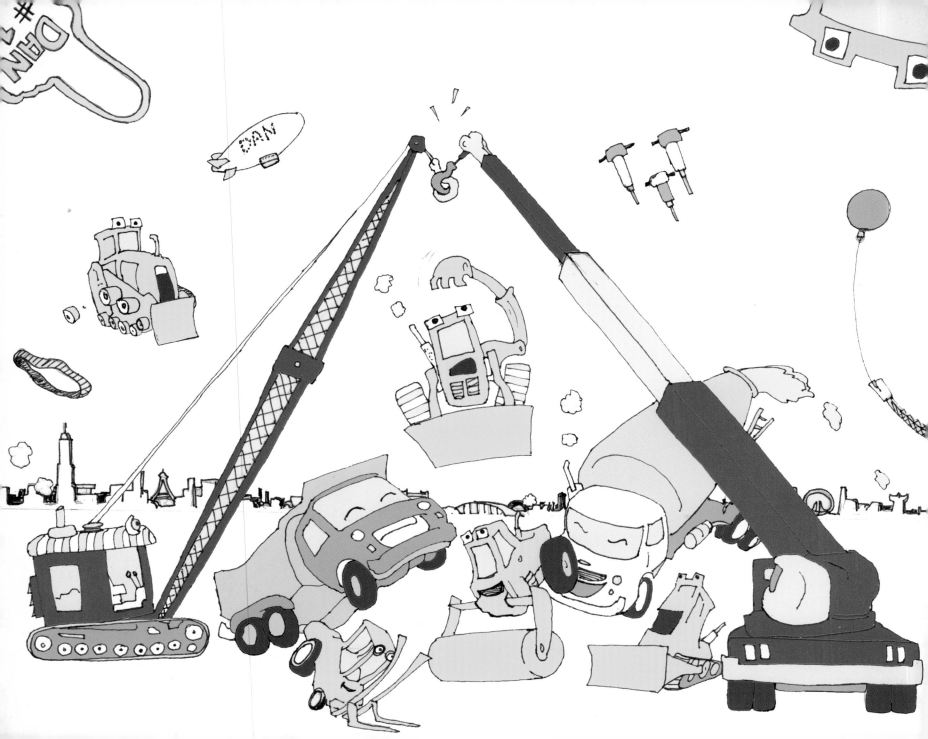

And when the site was clear, and the workers and equipment were all safe, everyone cheered for Dan!

"Hip, hip, hooray!"

"Hip, hip, hooray!"

"Hip, hip, hooray!"

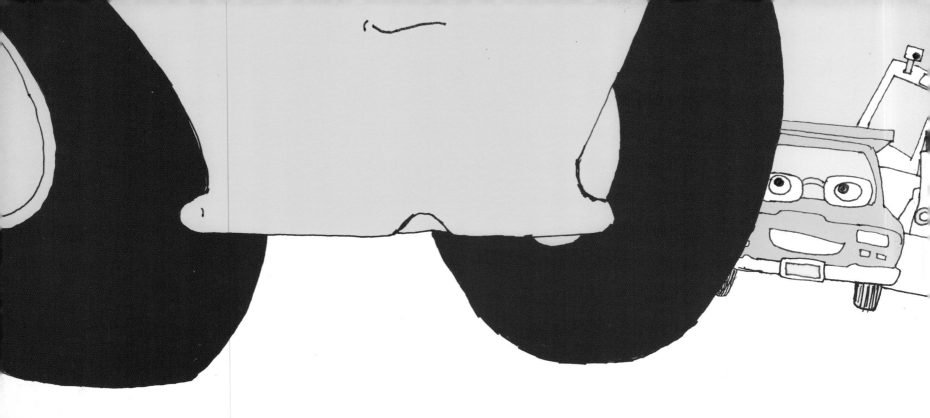

The construction crew foreman was so happy that Dan had saved the day—and the job—that he said, "Dan, you sure make quick work of all that dirt! How'd you like to join our crew and be our number one dump truck?"

And, at last, Dan was happy.

we jump in puddles

An imprint of Globe Pequot

Distributed by NATIONAL BOOK NETWORK

Text copyright © 2017 Chris Adams
Illustrations copyright © 2017 James Donahower
Cover and interior design by Piper F. Wallis

British Library Cataloguing in Publication Information Available

Library of Congress Cataloging-in-Publication Data Available

ISBN 978-1-63076-056-4 (cloth : alk. paper) —
ISBN 978-1-63076-057-1 (electronic)

♾ The paper used in this publication meets the minimum requirements of American National Standard for Information Sciences—Permanence of Paper for Printed Library Materials, ANSI/NISO Z39.48-1992.

Printed in Malaysia

Dedicated by the author to Cooper Adams

Dedicated by the illustrator to Jackson and Louis

The
Rhythm
of the
Rain

The rhythms and cycles of this wonderful world we live in are reflected
and echoed in our own selves and in those whom we love.
I dedicate this story to my wife Linda for her bravery and her sea-soul.

A TEMPLAR BOOK

First published in 2018 by Templar Books.
This paperback edition published in the UK in 2018 by Templar Books,
an imprint of Bonnier Books UK,
The Plaza, 535 King's Road, London, SW10 0SZ
Owned by Bonnier Books
Sveavägen 56, Stockholm, Sweden
www.templarco.co.uk
www.bonnierbooks.co.uk

ISBN 978-1-78741-015-2 (paperback)
ISBN 978-1-78741-412-9 (eBook)

Designed by Genevieve Webster
Edited by Alison Ritchie

Printed in China

FSC
www.fsc.org

MIX
Paper from
responsible sources
FSC® C104723

The Rhythm
of the
Rain

Grahame Baker-Smith

templar
books

Issac was playing in his favourite pool
on the side of his favourite mountain.
He felt spots of rain on his cheek and looked
up to see clouds turning dark above him.

As the rain poured down it made little streams that ran
out of Issac's pool. He emptied his jar of water into the pool too
and raced the laughing streams down the mountainside.

He watched as they joined the river that
ran past his home to plunge down a waterfall.

*Somewhere in all that tumbling
is my little jar of water*, Issac thought.

As the river went on it got deeper and wider.
Creatures came out of the woods to drink and to wash,
and fish leapt high out of the swelling water,
happy to see the rain.

On and on the river flowed,
winding through the country . . .

. . . winding through the city.
And everywhere it went, people and
creatures found a use for it.

Eventually it joined the great ocean.

Issac stood in his boat and waved goodbye to the river.

Where will my little jar of water go now? he wondered.

The ocean has many moods. It is home to many things.
A great whale opens its huge mouth to feed and swallows some
of the water from Issac's pool.

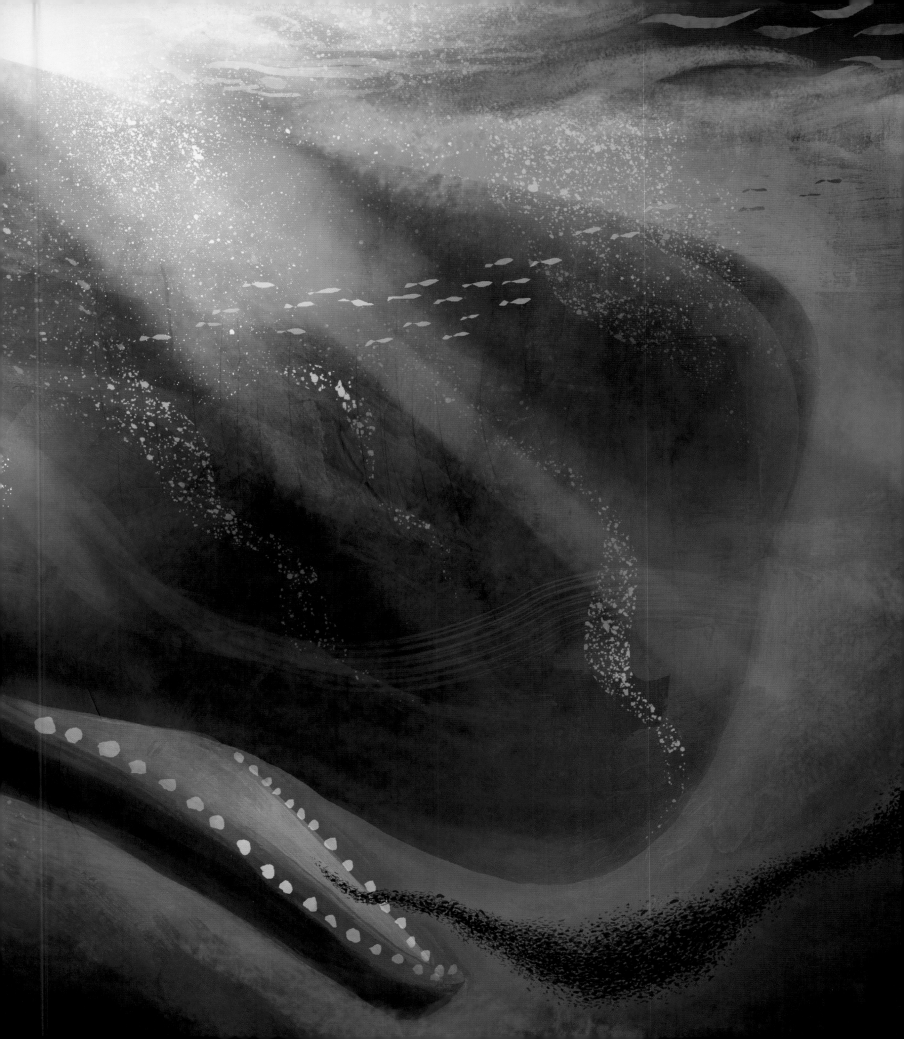

Later, by the light of the moon, the whale rises and blows a great fountain into the starry night. The water falls like rain back into the sea.

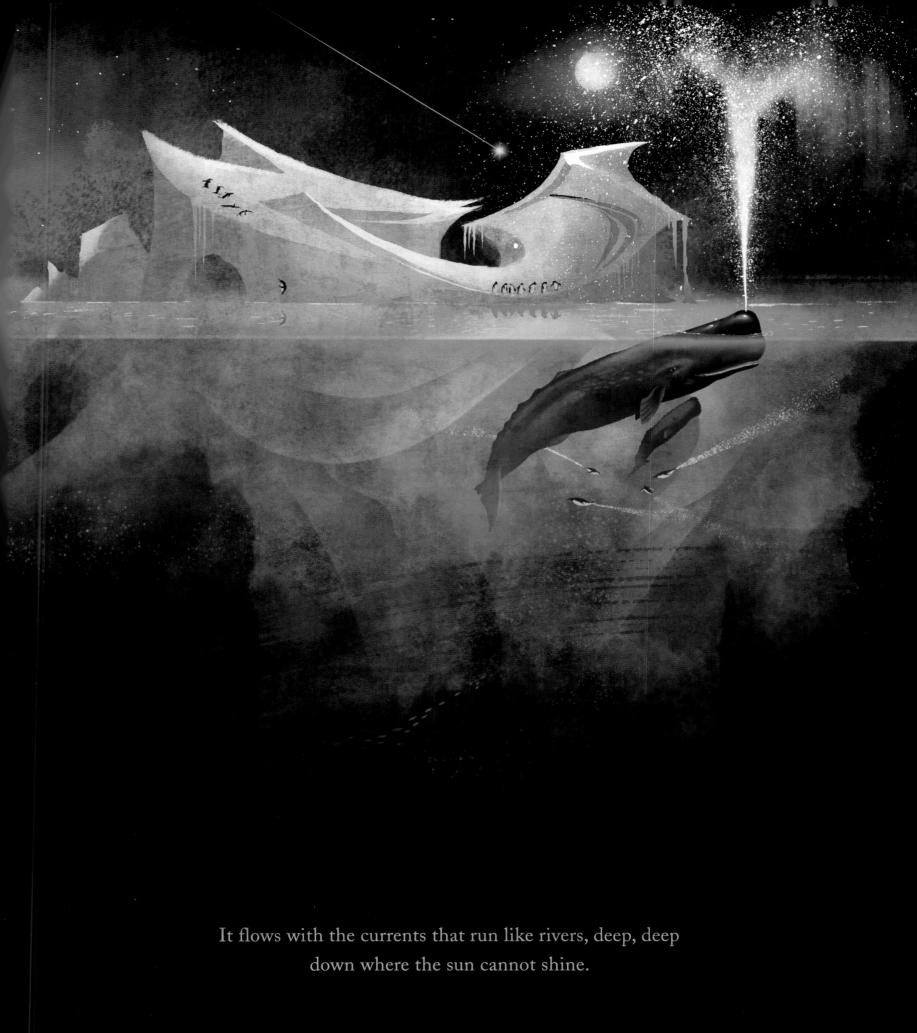

It flows with the currents that run like rivers, deep, deep
down where the sun cannot shine.

And rises to ride the storm all night long to another part of our blue water-world.

In the calm morning, the sun turns the waves golden.
The ocean steams beneath the heat and climbs as a mist into the sky.
The mist cools and gathers into a cloud that floats over a mountain
in a country far, far away from Issac's pool.

The clouds let go their gift of water.
They fill the pool where a little girl plays.

Cassi has been thirsty for days,
and she drinks gratefully.

Down the mountain the river runs.
Where it goes, the earth turns green. Elephants and giraffe,
flamingoes and zebra celebrate the return of the rain.

On and on the river runs . . .

Back to the sea . . .

. . . where a giant squid,
surprised by a shark . . .

. . . cleverly creates a cloud of ink,
and sucking in the sea,
jets away undercover to safety.

Once more – as it has done for millions of years –
the sun heats the ocean, and the water rises as steam
into the sky where it forms into clouds.
Once more – as it has done for millions of years –
the rain falls on the land.

And thirsty flowers draw the
wandering water into themselves,
waving like bright flags around
the pool where Issac plays.